The Caves of Qumran

FOCUS ON THE FAMILY PRESENTS

— ADVENTURES IN —

ODYSSEY

NEW SERIES

The Caves of Qumran

MARSHAL YOUNGER

{Based on the teleplay by Jeffrey Learned}

TYNDALE KIDS

TYNDALE HOUSE PUBLISHERS, INC.
WHEATON, ILLINOIS

Visit Tyndale's exciting Web site at www.tyndale.com

Visit Tyndale's exciting Web site for kids at www.cool2read.com

Designed by Julie Chen

Edited by Linda Piepenbrink

This novel is a work of fiction. Names, characters, places, and incidents are either the
product of the author's imagination or are used fictitiously. Any resemblance to actual events,
locales, organizations, or persons, living or dead, is entirely coincidental and beyond the
intent of either the author or publisher.

ISBN 1-56179-929-7

Printed in the United States of America

06   05   04   03   02   01
9   8   7   6   5   4   3   2   1

Contents

one

Out of the Shadows

STANLEY MARTIN had waited his entire life for this moment. Six miserable years of college, 14 unsuccessful archaeology trips searching for ancient artifacts and fossils—but this made it all worth it. Back in college, Stanley had endured ongoing ridicule from classmates and other archaeologists who made him the object of bad archaeology jokes. ("How many Stanley Martins does it take to search for the Red Sea Scrolls? Answer: 250. 249 to comb the entire area and one to realize they are actually at the *Dead* Sea.")

Even after earning his college degree, he didn't get much respect from his peers or professors. They didn't think he was cut out for archaeology. After all, he had trouble finding the prize at the bottom of a cereal box!

It wasn't that he didn't try to be a good archaeologist. He was sure he was the hardest worker of them all. He just had not been able to get a break.

Until now. This time he had been able to team up with his younger cousin, the respected Dr. Sara Norton, herself an archaeologist who had already discovered many important artifacts in her short career. Now she was trying to find perhaps an even greater artifact (the mysterious treasure of Pierre LeRue). Stanley had begged her to take him on the expedition and, reluctantly, out of family obligation, she allowed him to tag along.

Stanley loosened his tie with one hand and held a torch with the other as he walked through the ancient passageway of a cave at Qumran (pronounced KOOM-ron) near the Dead Sea. He was breathless with anticipation as he looked at the hieroglyphics on the wall. He knew these pictures were part of an ancient language, but he couldn't read them.

This will show my teachers, he thought. *If they could see me now* . . . He stumbled on the jagged rocks beneath the imitation-leather dress shoes he'd insisted on wearing with his suit. All those rugged archaeology clothes just didn't suit him.

Dr. Sara Norton had on traditional digging gear (khakis and hiking boots). She lifted her torch to read the hieroglyphics. The flickering light revealed large stone blocks, coated with cobwebs, lining the dark passage-way. Carved pictures and foreign symbols covered the walls. Dr. Norton smiled, obviously understanding some of the meaning of the pictures. Stanley didn't have a clue.

Dr. Norton moved on. Stanley followed like a faithful dog. They had to duck their heads as the passageway shrunk before them. They came to a fork in the tunnel. "Let's split up. You go that way," she said. She spoke with a British accent.

Stanley hesitated and swallowed a lump in his throat. He didn't particularly want to split up. There were, in fact, spiders in there, as well as who knows what 2,000-year-old creatures. Then again, maybe this would give him the opportunity to find the treasure first.

"Turn on your walkie-talkie," Dr. Norton said as they began to walk in separate directions. Stanley turned it on and headed into another passageway.

✳   ✳   ✳

It seemed to grow darker and stuffier the deeper Dr. Norton moved into the cave. It also began to smell like things that had not seen air or light in thousands of years. Who knows what had died in this place? Until this point, Dr. Norton had been so focused on reaching the treasure that she had not given any thought to the danger she could be facing. Now, as she walked deeper into this underground labyrinth—without Stanley by her side and with the stagnant smells all around her—she began to glance in other directions and to notice the strange shapes and sounds around her.

She heard an echo—a strange, unnatural sound that bounced off each wall and made her shudder. *What was that?* She swung the torch around quickly to see what had made the sound, but she saw nothing. She raised her two-way radio to her lips. "Stanley?" she whispered nervously. There was no response. "Stanley?" Still nothing. "Stanley!" she yelled. "Are you all right? Come in, *Stanley!*"

"I read you, Sara." Stanley's voice finally came through.

Sara breathed a sigh of relief. "Are you OK?"

"I'm fine," came his reply.

✳   ✳   ✳

Stanley was in the other passageway, wiping off his dress shoes with a handkerchief. He had stepped into some muddy water. He knelt down and lowered his torch to reveal a puddle that completely blocked his path.

"Are you sure?" Sara's voice sounded out over Stanley's radio. Seeing no way around the puddle, he tested the depth of the water with a walking stick. The stick hit solid earth less than an inch below the puddle's surface. He realized he would have to get his shoes muddy again, but he didn't see any other options.

He lifted the radio to his lips. "I'm simply trying to navigate my way across a small little puddle. . . ."

He stepped forward into the middle of the puddle. He felt for the ground but didn't find it. His foot continued downward. Suddenly he plunged in, sinking into the muddy water up to his neck. He flailed around, trying to find his footing. Finally Stanley reached the edge of the pool and dragged himself out.

He shook himself off and momentarily mourned the destruction of a perfectly good thirty-dollar polyester suit. He took off his suit coat and wrung it out between his hands. Dirty water spilled out onto the ground.

Stanley's radio sputtered on. "Stanley, I don't think we should've split up," said Sara's static-muffled voice. "I just heard a strange noise."

Am I detecting panic in my cousin's voice? Stanley wondered. Tossing his dripping suit coat aside, he felt a surge of manly strength. *I'd better comfort the poor damsel in distress!* he thought.

"Don't worry, Sara," he said into his radio. "There's nothing to be afraid of. There's no reason to develop a case of the heebie-jee—"

He suddenly stepped into a thick veil of cobwebs. He threw his arms upward, and the webs entrapped his body. He panicked, his arms flapping wildly. "Aaaaaaaaahhhhh!"

His radio cut on. "Stanley?" Sara called.

Stanley jumped around frantically. The more he struggled, the more he became entangled in the cobwebs. He flipped around, doing a full cartwheel into a wall, hitting his head, and landing on his backside.

"Oof!"

"Stanley! What's happening?!"

Stanley brushed the cobwebs off his face and scrambled for his radio. With all the composure he could muster, he replied, "Nothing. Just taking a little breather."

"Why were you screaming?" came Sara's voice. "Were you making fun of me?"

Stanley had to think quickly. "Yes. I mean, no." Thinking quickly wasn't one of Stanley's strengths. "I was just . . . testing the . . . echo amplitude of these walls."

"The echo amplitude?"

"Yes," he said, clearing his throat. "Something I learned in an archaeology course. These walls have excellent echo amplitude. Some of the best I've heard."

"Well, I don't know about echo amplitude, Stanley, but I think we should concentrate on the treasure. But I've got this strange feeling we're not alone in here."

Stanley was determined not to let fear get to him this time. Once, three years ago, he had missed out on discovering the scepter of an ancient king because he was scared off by a group of "religious zealots with guns," who turned out to be wandering shepherds with walking sticks. While Stanley had been hiding from the shepherds, another archaeologist swooped in and found the scepter. His friends and colleagues had never let Stanley hear the end of that one.

So Stanley had some bad memories to erase. He knew he could get to the treasure this time as long as he wasn't afraid. He had to be strong.

Stanley leaned over to tie his shoe and pick up his walking stick. Without realizing it, he nudged a protruding brick with his backside, pushing it into the wall. The wall began to revolve, revealing an ancient coffin, called a sarcophagus. It tipped forward, causing the top half of its lid to swing open. A lifeless mummy fell forward at the waist, its arms unfolded as if to reach for Stanley. He was still tying his shoe, unaware of the mummy behind him.

"I promise you, Sara," Stanley said into his walkie-talkie, "that besides Pierre LeRue, no one has been in here for over a thousand years. And if we're going to find whatever it is he hid in here, then we shouldn't be wasting our time chasing shadows."

He stood up, releasing the brick and causing the mummy to slide back in place and the wall to revolve again. Hearing rumbling, he stood frozen for a moment, then spun around just as the wall closed and there was nothing left to see.

"I'm sure you're right," Sara said. "No need to chase shadows."

But as soon as Stanley had finished reassuring Sara, he heard something else rather unsettling—a splash, as if someone had fallen into the puddle that he had just pulled himself out of. But the sound was too far away for that. He raised his torch to look back down the passageway and saw nothing. But there was no doubt in his mind that something was back there.

Sara's voice called again, startling him. "I'd still feel a whole lot better if you came over here."

This sounded like a great idea to Stanley, who was definitely wishing he were near Sara rather than near whatever was lurking behind him.

"Yes, all right," he said, trying to make it sound as though he were doing this for her benefit. "I'll be there as soon as I . . ."

His words trailed off as he heard a sound that could not be confused with anything else.

Footsteps.

✳   ✳   ✳

Sara, on the other hand, let her fear go and continued forward down the corridor. She studied the walls, the hieroglyphics still dominating almost every square

8

inch. But then something caught her eye. There was an inscription that was much different from the other wall carvings. It was a message written in French, and it was alongside the letters I-X-O-Y-E—the Greek word for *fish*. Sara knew it also was a Christian symbol. Each letter had special meaning: *I* for "Jesus," *X* for "Christ," *O* for "God," *Y* for "Son," and *E* for "Savior." The only way these letters would be on the walls of this cave was if some French Christian had been here first.

"LeRue," she said with a smile. She knew she was on the right track. She hurried along, both in anticipation and with the fleeting thought that she wanted to lay her eyes on the treasure before Stanley or anyone else arrived. She was not normally this competitive, but this treasure was special, and she wanted to get to it first. The air was getting thinner as Dr. Norton descended deeper underground. Her torch sputtered and lit up only ten feet of darkness in front of her; behind her, it was completely dark.

Suddenly she heard a strange moan from behind. She spun around, waving her torch back and forth to see everything around her. But the torch lit up only a few feet. "Stanley?" An eerie silence filled the corridor. There was no air flowing, no rock creaking above her, no water dripping. Just silence. She was afraid to move.

It is just the wind blowing over the cave opening, she

thought. *Wind makes a moaning noise. Or perhaps it is Stanley checking the "echo amplitude."*

She decided to keep moving, trying to ignore all the fears that were floating through her mind. As the passageway turned a corner in front of her, she hesitantly followed it. She peered around the corner, and what she saw made every ounce of fear melt away.

"Oh, my," she whispered in awe.

At the end of the passageway a crate lay on the ground. On it was inscribed IXOYE. It was an ordinary wooden box, but to Sara it seemed made of pure gold. "It's here," she said breathlessly to herself. Drawn like a magnet, she approached it. She was in a trance, unaware of anything around her. Without thinking, she set her radio and torch on the ground and fixed her gaze on the crate.

While in this trance she missed her cousin's warnings over the radio. "Sara! Sara, you were right!" came Stanley's unheeded words over the radio. "There is someone—or something—else in here!"

Stepping away from the torch and the radio, Sara moved like a zombie toward the crate. She felt her hands tremble in anticipation as she knelt before it, wiping her hands on her shirt before preparing to open it.

From the radio came Stanley's shout: "Sara! Run, before it's too—nooooo!" The radio abruptly cut out to static.

Sara opened the crate, its contents barely visible. She reached down into it and felt around. Her hand brushed up against a parchment. Her heart leaped. She pulled it out into the light of the torch, which was still on the ground behind her.

"The final piece!" she said.

Her trance was broken by a strange, dragging sound, followed by a thud right behind her. She turned around and scrambled to find her torch. "Stan?" She looked down and saw Stanley lying on the ground, bound and gagged. His eyes were frantic, and his screams were muffled by the gag.

Still on her knees, she peered into the darkness. The torch was gone, but she could still see some light from it. She heard a sound like cracking knuckles. A figure came out of the shadows and approached her, holding the torch.

"No! Please, nooooo!"

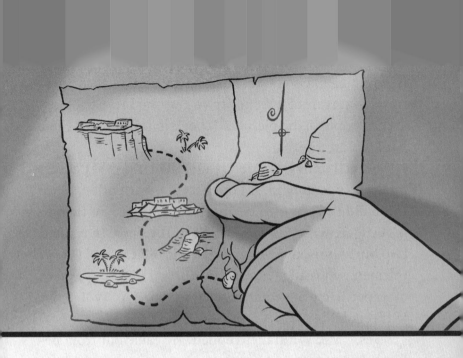

IT HAD been a slow day at Whit's End, the most popular kid hangout in Odyssey. John Avery Whittaker, owner and operator of the ice-cream shop and known as "Whit" to most adults, was standing behind the front counter, drawing a schematic of a new invention he had been thinking about. His employees, Eugene Meltsner and Connie Kendall, were arguing about whether or not Connie could handle the college load that Eugene was currently carrying.

Twelve-year-old Dylan Taylor, who rarely let a day go by without stopping in at Whit's End, was leafing through a magazine, gazing at all the beautiful people and the expensive stuff they owned. He imagined what it would be like to be able to buy cars and boats or anything you wanted whenever you wanted it. He looked at the people in the pictures. Their smiles matched their bank accounts—big.

The bell above the door rang, signaling that a customer was coming in. It got everyone's attention, since there didn't appear to be anything better to do than to investigate who just came through the door. In walked two burly, unshaven men dressed in old clothes. One of the men, who called himself Rudy, was carrying a piece of paper. He glanced at it, then asked, "Are you John Whittaker?"

"Yes," Mr. Whittaker replied. He came out from behind the counter.

"We've got some stuff for you."

"Stuff?"

"Yeah, somebody donated a truckload."

"Donated? But . . . we're not a charity."

The two men exchanged looks, as if they were searching for a response. "This person just likes the work you do here in this place and wanted to be nice and give you some stuff."

"What person?"

They looked at each other again. Then Rudy said, "The donor wishes to remain una . . . unamana . . . mus."

"Anonymous?" Eugene said.

"Yeah. That's it."

Mr. Whittaker scratched his chin. "Hmmm. Strange. I suppose we could go look at it."

They all headed for the door.

✳   ✳   ✳

Mr. Whittaker lifted the door on the back of the truck, and they all peered inside. The truck was full of antiques—lamps, chairs, wall hangings, pictures—all things that would fit very nicely into the Victorian-style mansion that was Whit's End.

Whit was delighted. Some of the antiques took him back to his younger days as a child in North Carolina. Dylan thought the old stuff was very cool and secretly wondered how much money it would sell for.

Whit went back to Rudy. "Isn't there an address you could give me? I'd love to thank the person."

"No address."

"Maybe I could just give you a letter and you could hand deliver it."

"No letters."

Whit thought this was very odd. Connie, Eugene, and Dylan were on the truck sifting through the goods, and Whit called them out. "Hey, let's make sure we get a record of everything," he said. "Hang on. Let me get my clipboard."

Rudy and his partner, whose name was Boris, put the things on the sidewalk in front of the shop. Eugene and

Dylan organized the loot on the sidewalk. Connie examined the items and told Whit, who had his clipboard ready, what to write down.

"OK," Connie said as she picked up a triangular accordion-like object. "This item is an . . . inflator-type thingy dealy-bob. . . ."

Eugene walked over to assist her. "That, you poor helpless girl, is referred to as a bellows," he said proudly. "It is for stoking fires."

Whit wrote it down. Dylan handed Connie another strange object. "Let's see," Connie said, trying to seem confident but wrinkling her brows, "it looks to me like this . . . is . . . a small, little . . . devicelike object . . . for stapling . . . paper and stuff?"

Eugene chuckled to himself, then let out an exasperated sigh loud enough for Connie to hear it. "It is a telegraph transmitter, circa 1870."

Connie blew her hair out of her eyes, frustrated with Eugene's constantly showing her up.

Eugene looked at her with a slight grin. "Perhaps we should exchange jobs, Miss Kendall?"

"No thanks. I'm doing just fine. I'll get the next one," she said. She spoke too soon. Boris handed her a mangled mass of twisted metal, glass, and plastic. Two spheres that looked like misshapen eyeballs peered out from the middle. It actually startled her when she first laid eyes on it.

16

"Um . . . this is . . ." She hung her head down in defeat. "I don't know. Modern art?"

"Very impressive, Miss Kendall. That is precisely correct."

Connie looked pleasantly surprised as Eugene continued.

"The artist is Dieter Sergei, known for his abstract voice depicting the human condition. This piece is entitled *Man As a Vaporous Hole.*"

They all stared at it. "The eyes are looking at me," Connie said.

"That's art?" Dylan said.

One of the rusty eyeballs fell out of place and bounced on the ground. "Maybe we could melt it down for scrap metal," Eugene said.

The burly men had cleared the truck of everything, and Rudy came out with the last piece—an antique vase. Whit glanced at it and thought it could be very valuable, but apparently Rudy didn't value its worth as much as Whit did. He palmed the vase with his right hand and cocked it behind his head. "Hey, kid. Go long."

Rudy threw the vase like a football in Dylan's direction, but it was over his head. Like a wide receiver, he bolted to catch it, backpedaling and jumping over the objects they'd placed on the sidewalk. He hopped on top of a box to try to reach it, but the vase was sailing too far. It flew over his fingertips, shattering on the concrete behind him.

Whit, Connie, and Eugene gathered around the broken vase. "I'm sorry, Mr. Whittaker," Dylan said. "I tried to catch it."

"That's all right, Dylan. Those men were careless."

The truck's engine revved up, and the truck peeled out down the street without so much as a good-bye from the two men. It was out of sight in a matter of seconds.

"Apparently the movers understood their carelessness as well," Eugene said.

They all watched the smoke from the truck clear until Dylan shouted, "Hey, guys, look at this!"

From the base of the broken vase, he pulled out what appeared to be a piece of leather. He unfolded it gently. Three sides of it were straight, but the fourth side was jagged, as if it had been ripped. It had words and pictures on it. In the upper right-hand corner was a hand-drawn compass. And in the middle of it, below what appeared to be a picture of a mountain, was a large black *X*.

Dylan had seen these on television. He knew exactly what this was. "It's a treasure map!"

Whit leaned down to get a closer look. He recognized the words as French, and at the bottom he saw the letters *PL*. He had a hunch he knew what this was.

18

"Let's get all the stuff inside and then take a closer look. This could be something very valuable."

Dylan's eyes lit up.

Connie, Eugene, and Dylan ran faster than they had ever run before as they moved the antiques into the shop. When they were done, they gathered in the library and laid the map in front of them on a table. Parts of the map were blurred by age, but most of it was fairly easy to read. Eugene translated the French to himself. He had an idea of what the map could be as well.

Whit walked into the library with a history book about the Old World.

"Well?" Dylan asked impatiently. "Do you know what it is?"

"Do me a favor, Eugene," Whit said, enjoying keeping them in suspense. "Scan the map onto your computer."

Eugene took the map and booted up his computer.

Whit turned back to the group. "If it's authentic . . . , this could be the missing piece of a puzzle that's more than 200 years old."

"More than 200 years old?" Dylan asked.

"Unbelievable, isn't it?" Whit said. "What's even more amazing is that I believe its author may be the legendary adventurer Pierre LeRue."

"So that's what *PL* stands for," Eugene said, smacking himself on the head. "Pierre LeRue, of course."

"Who was Pierre LeRue?" Connie asked.

Whit opened the history book and pointed to the man's picture. "A French nobleman, an archaeologist, and a Christian. Many of his discoveries were items that have been very valuable to biblical studies. In fact, his work was what inspired my own interest in archaeology."

"Whoa," Dylan said. "Does anyone know about this map?"

Eugene took the liberty of answering this question. "Actually, the incomplete map is widely known in the archaeological community. It's a map of a cave in Qumran, which is near the Dead Sea. I'm pulling up the records right now, and if Mr. Whittaker is correct, this piece should make the map complete."

Dylan and Connie shifted in their seats so they could see the computer screen. On it were two halves of a map—one, the half that they had discovered hidden in the vase, and the other, the existing map. The two halves were morphing slowly and inching closer together.

Whit continued as they watched in awe. "LeRue's legend goes back to the late 1700s. The legends say that his map of Qumran leads to his greatest treasure of all. The only problem is, the part that shows where the treasure is has been missing for centuries. Many have searched, but it's never been found. If this piece fits, we could know the exact whereabouts of LeRue's greatest treasure!"

The two pieces of the map continued to come together. The scanner turned off, and the fragment locked into place. The half-pictures became a full picture. The half-words suddenly made sense. It was perfect.

"Whoa," Dylan said.

"Eureka!" Eugene said. "A perfect fit! It appears to be authentic."

"I can't believe it," Connie said, covering her mouth with her hand.

"It's real," Whit said, entranced by the screen. "Print it out, Eugene."

"Yes," he said, although several seconds went by before he could take his eyes off the screen.

"What are you gonna do?" Connie asked.

Whit pointed to an area of the map that showed some ancient buildings. Underneath them was the word *Qumran*. "I think I'm taking a trip to—" he pointed to Qumran—"right there."

"Really?" Connie asked. "Can I come?"

"Well . . ."

"Oh, I wanna come too," Dylan pleaded.

"I'm sure I could be of some assistance to you, Mr. Whittaker," Eugene said. "I have an extensive knowledge of archaeology."

"I can read French!" Connie shouted.

"You're literate in French, Miss Kendall?" Eugene asked.

Dylan wasn't about to be left out. "I can . . . um . . . I can . . . well, I found the map! I deserve to go."

"I'll tell you what," Whit said. "You can all come, as long as it's OK with your parents." He pointed to Dylan and Connie.

"Yes!" Dylan shouted.

Connie was out the door in seconds, ready to pack her bags. She needed a vacation.

❋ ❋ ❋

Mr. Whittaker took Dylan home and talked to his parents about the trip to Qumran. Mr. Whittaker was the most respected person in Odyssey, and there was no one his parents trusted more with their son than him. A trip with Whit would be an educational experience, teaching Dylan not only about history but about life. Dylan practically flew through the roof with excitement when his parents finally said yes. He was done packing his suitcase in about five milliseconds, even though the trip was not for another few days.

He couldn't sleep that night. Staring at the ceiling till past midnight, he asked himself many questions, but all of them had the same theme: How much? How much money would the treasure be worth? How much would Mr. Whittaker allow him to claim, since he was one of four people on the trip? *Whit's a fair man,* Dylan thought, *and I'm the one who discovered the map, anyway. I should probably get half of the money myself just for that.* Dylan reminded himself that Connie really didn't have anything to do with the treasure; she was just tagging along. And Eugene would be spouting off a lot of unnecessary facts and figures, so he really didn't deserve much of the loot.

Dylan wondered if the treasure was worth as much as a million dollars. He wondered what he would do with that much money, and the thought made him happy. He had always wanted a sailboat. He wondered how big of a sailboat he could get with a million dollars. It would practically be the *Titanic,* he bet.

He finally dozed off, with visions of boats and motorcycles and gold-plated skateboards dancing in his head.

DYLAN HAD been skeptical when Whit kept referring to their destination as the ancient land of Qumran. He understood that it was in the desert, not a city like Odyssey, but he still expected modern structures. He was sure there would be a mall or a Burger Boy nearby.

He was wrong. The city could have been transported here directly from 2,000 years ago. The houses were made of cracked, uneven stone with rectangular holes for doorways. People were buying and selling in an outdoor marketplace, where colorful awnings sprouted out of adobe storefronts and tall clay vases, jugs, and baskets lined the walls. Rickety carts with large circular wooden wheels held everything from rugs to vegetables. On one rug a snake charmer sat with his legs folded, playing a pipe. A cobra danced upward from inside a basket.

There were only a few things that betrayed that this was not actually the first century A.D. Most of those things were in and around Connie's luggage. Whit, Connie, Eugene, and Dylan had filled up their saddlebags with supplies and strapped them onto four camels. Three of the camels were traveling with ease. Connie's camel was trembling, its knees buckling under the weight of her overloaded bags.

They led their camels through the dense crowd of merchants and customers in the marketplace. People rushed about in a flurry of activity, like bees in a hive.

Dylan's eyes were like saucers. "Mr. Whittaker, this is amazing!"

Whit smiled and agreed. "I'm glad your parents let you come along. After all, this may be your one chance to see the Middle East firsthand."

Connie walked by the side of her camel that was away from the others, brushing up on her French using a French-English dictionary. She didn't want Eugene to see that she wasn't completely confident in her ability to translate for the group, since that was the reason she'd given for coming in the first place. So what if she'd only had one semester of high school French? In reality, she was dying to take pictures and show all her friends that she had been to the Middle East. She'd received a nice camera for Christmas and had eight rolls of film to burn up; she planned to use them all.

She put away her dictionary and ran up in front of Eugene. "OK, stand still. Somebody needs to document this trip."

"And how, pray tell, do you plan to chronicle this historical excursion?"

She forcefully jerked Eugene in close to her side and held the camera at arm's length in front of them. "Say cheeeese!" She snapped the photo before Eugene could resist. "That's a keeper," she said.

"Yes, I'm sure you'll win some kind of local photo contest," Eugene replied with a sigh.

✲　　✲　　✲

Someone who wasn't interested in joking around was nearby. A dark, cloaked figure stood behind Whit and the others, studying their every move, waiting for the right moment. He ducked in behind the corner of a shop and watched. As Whit and the gang parked their camels and continued through the marketplace, the man in the cloak quickly snuck over to the camels. This was the moment he had been waiting for.

It was Whit's camel he was interested in. His eyes darted from left to right to check if anyone was looking; then he began to rifle through Whit's saddlebag. He found a few things he didn't need—socks, underwear, a flashlight—but then he found something he could definitely use. He pulled out his hand and beheld a passport bearing the name John Avery Whittaker. Whit's photo, a shot of him looking like he was not ready for the camera to flash, stared up at him.

The cloaked man put the passport into his pocket and decided to go ahead and swipe the entire saddlebag, in case Whit carried a journal in there or something. He peered out from between two camels. He would just casually move away from them now. . . .

Suddenly Connie's camel shifted under the weight of her heavy luggage and moved its foot, stepping full on the man's toe.

"Aaaaaaahhhhhh!"

Dylan was the only one who heard the scream. The noise from the marketplace was deafening, and apparently the people around him were used to loud noises because no one moved but him. He thought the sound came from the direction of the camels. Dylan moved to look between the camels and saw someone there—someone in a dark cloak. It looked like the person was stealing one of their saddlebags!

Dylan ran toward him, but one camel moved to block his vision. "Hey!" he yelled.

Dylan whipped around the back of the camel. "Hey,

the caves of qumran

what do you think—" But the person in the dark cloak was gone. "Where'd he go?" he said to himself.

Whit came up behind him. "Where did who go, Dylan?"

"Someone was going through our saddlebags!"

"What?! Are you sure?"

"Positive. He was dressed in black."

Whit scanned the bags as Connie and Eugene joined the group. "Check your things," he told them. "Someone may have been trying to steal our supplies."

"What?" Connie said.

"Pilferers?" Eugene exclaimed.

They all surveyed their things and found that only one bag was missing.

"I think we can do without everything that was in that bag," Whit said. "But I would recommend everyone keeping a sharp eye on their belongings. Let's get going."

Connie, Dylan, and Eugene scanned the area for suspicious people the rest of the trip. They trusted no one. But they failed to lay eyes on the one who was following them out of the city and into the desert.

❋   ❋   ❋

The map they were following didn't show actual distances on it, so no one really had much of an idea how long this trip would be. It was already way too long for

Dylan, who got bored almost immediately when they reached the edge of the desert. There were no street signs to read, no interesting buildings, just sand. Lots of sand. And sweat from riding under the hot sun. Dylan had a lot of time to think about all the things he would buy with his share of the treasure, but he had already gone through his list in bed the other night.

Dylan sped up on his camel to ride alongside Mr. Whittaker. He figured he would make the time go faster by making conversation. Whit was holding up the map to compare it to the desert horizon and to check if anything in his path matched.

"Mr. Whittaker, why are you so interested in this Pierre guy?"

"Well, the reason this trip is more important than just finding an artifact is that Pierre LeRue was a man of God. Hopefully, by finding his treasure, I'll understand more about his life and his faith."

"What happened to him?"

"LeRue was working at an archaeological site in some cave outside of Qumran in the late eighteenth century. But then the revolution broke out back home in France."

"The French Revolution?"

"Right. You see, for many years the king of France had been persecuting many of his countrymen—crushing their freedom. Soldiers would force people from their own homes at gunpoint. Entire families were mistreated."

"Why would the king do that?"

"He tried to destroy anything—including the Bible—that took power away from him. He had Bibles burned in bonfires, and Christians were killed if they were caught reading the Bible or trying to protect their beliefs in any way. Many good people lost their lives because they wouldn't give up their faith in God."

"Whoa," Dylan said.

"Eventually, because of his importance, LeRue was ordered to return home to France. And that was the last time anyone ever heard from him."

By this time, both Connie and Eugene were also enraptured by this story and had moved alongside Whit's camel. "Well, what do you think LeRue hid in the caves of Qumran?" Connie asked.

"I don't know. But whatever it was, it must have been important."

✳   ✳   ✳

The desert was so barren and lifeless, the gang never suspected there was someone else out there in the sand. Watching them through a spyglass, the man in black stood behind them on a rocky hill.

With all the professional expertise he could muster, he watched intently, so focused on the camel riders below that he didn't see the tumbleweed blow toward him—and hit him square in the face. He lowered the spyglass and spit out barbs of tumbleweed.

This was something that could happen only to Stanley Martin.

Stanley's black cloak blew open in the blustery desert wind. Underneath it, he wore a brand-new forty-dollar suit and tie. Now that he was in the role of private investigator instead of archaeologist, he would solve this case in style.

After the map had been stolen from Sara and him while they were in the cave, Stanley had begun a desperate search to find the thief and get the map back. He had not gotten a good look at the person who had tied him up and taken the map; the man had concealed himself behind a cloak. But at least the thief had not tried to hurt either Stanley or Sara. Instead, he'd just taken the map and run away. As soon as Sara had untied Stanley they followed after the cloaked criminal, but they never found him.

Days later, Stanley got a call. It was an anonymous tip from someone who called himself Mr. X. He told Stanley that Whit had stolen the map and was on his way to Qumran. Mr. X hung up before Stanley could inquire further.

Stanley wanted to tell Sara but decided not to. This would be his chance to show himself worthy of respect in the archaeological community. If he retrieved the map without her, he would be her hero. He would probably be the cover story in every archaeological magazine in the world.

Trying to be a true private investigator, he felt he must record every thought on his microcassette recorder. He lifted it to his lips. "Log 0-1-6. It seems that my informant, Mr. X, was correct. I've personally identified John Avery Whittaker as the culprit who has the stolen map in his possession."

He pulled off his hood, replaced it with a sophisticated fedora hat, and continued. "Four, I repeat, four suspects are heading west! The leader is this Whittaker fellow. I'm proceeding with caution." He approached his camel, although the thought of riding such a repulsive animal made him squeamish. But it was the only way to keep up with the suspects. "Don't worry, Sara. Now that Stanley Martin is on the job, you'll get your map back!"

He lifted his leg to the stirrup on the camel's side. "Follow those tracks, you dirty beast!" He slapped the hindquarters of the camel, and it took off.

Without him.

*　　*　　*

Whit and the gang were not the only ones being watched in the desert. Rudy and Boris, the movers, peered through binoculars and watched Stanley get left behind by his camel, his foot still in the air where the stirrup had been. A trail of supplies littered the sand behind the camel.

"What an idiot," Rudy said. He and Boris were situated on an even higher rocky hill, watching the clumsy antics of Stanley Martin. Rudy enjoyed this show, but Stanley was not the one he was called on to follow. He was tracking the foursome in front of Stanley.

"They're still on the trail," Rudy said, holding a cellular phone in his left hand and the binoculars in his right. "Only there's one complication," Rudy said into the phone.

The voice on the other end of the line said, "What is it?"

"Some guy named Stanley Martin."

The voice did not seem concerned. "And the problem would be . . . ?"

Rudy and Boris stood up and made their way to their own form of transportation—a black, all-terrain four-wheel drive vehicle that was perfect for the sand. They hopped in and Rudy hung up the phone. He no longer needed it.

"Well, sir," Rudy continued, "it appears this Martin guy is following Whittaker."

"Don't worry, gentlemen," Mr. X said from the backseat. "Everything is going according to plan."

Rudy turned the key and the vehicle roared to life. "Well, should we keep following Whittaker?"

"Yes, and don't let them out of your sight!"

❋ ❋ ❋

The caves of Qumran were more breathtaking than any of them had imagined. Enormous cliffs rose up from the sand like skyscrapers. The sides were riddled with hundreds of small caves. *And in one of those,* Dylan thought, *is a treasure*.

Whit dismounted his camel, and the rest of the gang followed suit. He examined the map very closely, looking puzzled as he stared up at a solid wall of rock. A large round stone leaned up against it.

"According to LeRue, this is the spot," he said.

Dylan couldn't imagine that Whit was right about this. There were so many caves all around them, and Mr. Whittaker picked a wall of rock as the entranceway. He made the obvious statement. "But Mr. Whittaker, there's no cave here."

"Can someone translate this clue?" Whit asked, handing the map to whoever was game.

Eugene stepped over quickly. "Certainly."

Connie cut him off, anxious to prove her worth. "I can do it, Whit." She glanced at the French words. They looked more foreign than she would have preferred, but she took a deep breath and began to try to translate them to English. "'The treasure is . . . better than a stone.' That doesn't seem right, does it? I'll try again." She studied the map more closely.

Eugene folded his arms and tapped his fingers.

"'The gift,'" Connie continued, "'smells like butter'?"

Eugene was losing patience. "Miss Kendall, please let—"

"No, wait! I can get this! 'The butter is bitter.' Bitter! It's bitter. No, the bitter butter is better!" She was losing control. "The better butter is bigger! The big better butter is better bottled with bubbles!"

Eugene calmly stepped forward, placing his hand on her shoulder like a baseball manager giving the bad news to a pitcher that it's time to bring in relief. "Allow me to relieve us of this misery."

Eugene grasped the map and cleared his throat. "The clue reads, 'If the better treasure you would own, your first small task, to roll the stone.'"

"Oh, yeah, that's what I was going to say next," said Connie, forcing a chuckle.

Whit walked up to the stone and began to push on it, but it was obviously not going to budge. "Move the stone?" Dylan said. "It's gotta weigh a ton!"

Eugene corrected him. "Actually, judging from its estimated mass and density, 2.5 tons is more accurate."

Whit pushed on the stone some more, but to no avail. He stepped back and studied it from top to bottom.

"When it came to hidden treasure, LeRue was known for his harmless tricks. In fact, he often used them to teach valuable lessons. There's probably something here that we're just not seeing."

Whit scoured the stone with his hands, trying to find just the right spot to push. The other three stepped forward to help, but they couldn't see any point in helping push, since the task was obviously not reliant on strength. Even ten people couldn't move this stone.

Whit lowered his shoulder against the rock and tried again, but his footing gave way. "I need some leverage," he said.

He looked down and spotted a smaller rock next to his foot. He placed his foot on the smaller rock to push off it.

But when he put pressure on the smaller rock, it began to slide out from under his foot. Dylan watched as it slid away to reveal a small peg embedded in the ground beneath it. Released from the weight of the small stone, the peg began to rise.

The ground shook a bit, and Whit stopped pushing on the rock. He and his companions noticed the peg, then saw something else. A small pedestal, about the size of a TV tray, was rising from the ground directly in front of the large boulder. It stopped when it had risen four inches from the ground. The group huddled around the pedestal.

"What is it?" Dylan asked.

"It may be some kind of trigger," Whit said.

Without hesitation, Whit moved forward and stepped on the middle of the pedestal. It sank back into the ground under his weight. The ground shook again, and dirt and pebbles fell from around the boulder's circumference. The group backed away from it at once. Slowly the boulder rolled aside as if it were a bowling ball, revealing the entrance to a large cave.

"Whoa," said Dylan, his mouth wide open.

four

The Hall of Coins

THE CAVE was so dark that the four could barely see inside the entrance. The mouth was oblong and large enough to walk through without bending over. Connie pulled out her camera and shot about 20 pictures in a row. She had a history of good shots not turning out quite right. She had to make sure she got at least one decent picture. She pulled down an enormous backpack from the camel and put the camera inside. She fit the backpack over her shoulders and was ready to go inside.

Dylan wanted to jump right in too, but hesitated because he would be stepping into almost complete darkness. Whit took the lead and moved toward the mouth of the cave but stopped and turned around at the entrance. He instructed, "Be careful. These caves are extremely old, and the walls may be unstable. Also, some of LeRue's booby traps might be awaiting us. Keep your eyes peeled."

"Nice colloquialism," Eugene said to himself.

The darkness enveloped them as soon as they made it inside the entrance. "Mr. Whittaker, do you have the flashlights?" Dylan asked.

"I did," he replied, "but unfortunately they were in the stolen bag."

An extinguished torch was sticking out of a hole in the wall of the cave. "How fortunate," Eugene said, pulling it out and placing it on the ground in front of him. He pulled from his vest two flint rocks he had brought along in case this very scenario occurred. Actually, the flint rocks would have been a last resort if the batteries in the flashlights went out. "No need to fear," Eugene said, "for I am prepared with a backup plan. With my survival skills still intact, I should be able to give us some much needed light with this relic from times past."

He struck the rocks together in hopes of setting off sparks that would light the torch. He slapped them together with precision but only produced a few measly sparks.

At the same time, Connie was digging into her backpack. She plunged her hand down beyond the sunscreen, mosquito repellent, and sunglasses, and grasped an industrial flashlight nearly as big as a fire hydrant.

"Hmmm. Hard to see," Eugene said, continuing his fruitless attempt to start a fire.

Connie turned on her flashlight, and suddenly Eugene was bathed in enough light to illuminate a football game. "Does this help?" she said.

"Why yes, Miss Kendall, thank you," said Eugene, so wrapped up in his task of creating a fire that he didn't realize Connie held all the light they would need.

"Connie," said Whit, "shine that light over here, please." He pointed to the cave wall, where an inscription was carved.

"It's in French, but I think I can get this one," Connie said, directing the flashlight beam on the wall. "I believe it says, 'Jeremiah 13:16.' Yeah, that's it. Jeremiah 13:16."

Connie was proud that she had finally contributed something. She remembered that Jeremiah in French was *Jérémie,* which was very similar to Jeremiah in English, and numbers were exactly the same in both languages.

"What does Jeremiah 13:16 say?" Dylan asked.

"I know that one," Whit said. "That verse says, 'Give glory to the Lord your God before He causes darkness, and before your feet stumble.' Hmmm. Feet stumble. I wonder if that's a clue."

Eugene, still intent on getting a fire started, finally struck up enough of a spark to set the torch aflame. "Eureka!" The torch lit up the ground around him. But his work was not completely needless, because his torch illuminated an area that the flashlight had not yet hit.

And Whit noticed something. "Look!" He pointed to where Eugene sat. There was a trip wire running along the ground, about an inch high. "It's part of a booby trap. Everybody step over it carefully—don't touch the wire!"

The group lined up single file and tiptoed over the wire, exaggerating their steps to make sure they didn't touch it.

* * *

Stanley Martin limped along, his head bowed to cut through the driving sand. His suit coat was tied around his head with his necktie so that he looked like a sheik. He would sacrifice style for practicality at this point. He had to protect his neck and head from the scorching heat, which had already parched his throat and burned every square inch of exposed flesh on his body. As he battled the strong wind, the sand felt like tiny needles flying into his face.

He had very little strength left in his tired, dehydrated body. The only thing that kept him moving was the trail of supplies that the camel had left behind. Every 50 yards or so, Stanley would come across another bag he had packed. In one of them, he knew he had packed a canteen filled with water. If he found the bag with the canteen, it would be enough to last him another quarter mile or so, and that might be just enough to get to Whittaker. Every black bag in the distance was new hope for him, but so far he hadn't found the right bag. Now he saw another one. It was a bag certainly big enough to carry the canteen, and he could already taste the water. It had to be the right one. He had already sifted through four bags, and he'd only packed six. This had to be the one. If it wasn't, he didn't think he could make it any farther. He felt like he had no fluid left in his body; the sun had dried it all up.

He stumbled to the bag, his strides getting faster in anticipation. He picked it up, unzipped it, and tore through the contents: shaving cream . . . shoe polish . . . extra cuff links . . . nose hair trimmer . . . no canteen. He half considered sucking on the shaving cream can, but he stopped himself. It was over. He fell to his knees and pulled the tape recorder out of his pocket. "Stanley Martin's last will and testament. I do bequeath my lava lamp to . . ."

Suddenly he heard something. He lifted his head and

for one moment thought he was seeing a mirage. Then he looked more closely. It was his camel, along with four other camels. They were tied up in front of an open cave.

He smiled and felt a sudden burst of energy. Clicking off his microcassette recorder, he pulled out Mr. Whittaker's passport picture and spoke bluntly to it. "Whittaker, you've met your match."

*　　*　　*

Led by Connie's flashlight and Eugene's torch, the group moved slowly through the passageway, keeping a close eye on the walls and ground to find any clues or traps. The passageway widened to form a small chamber, which broke off to the left and right. To the left was a long hallway that led into darkness. To the right was a small hole, like an unfinished tunnel. On the wall in front of them was an inscription written in French. This was the first decision they had to make. "Oh, man," Dylan said. "Which way, Mr. Whittaker?"

"I'm not quite sure," he replied, studying the inscription.

Connie's attention was drawn to the hallway to the left. She noticed something sparkling in the middle of the darkness. Without a word, she moved toward it as if it were magnetic. She shone the light in, but beyond the edge of the light she saw something peering out from the darkness—100 pairs of eyes!

Whit noticed her moving away from the group. His mouth opened in terror. "Connie! Don't go in there!"

Connie jumped back, then froze in place. She was afraid to move, for fear that movement would bother the creatures that were staring at her.

Whit ran after Connie when she didn't answer him. He heard her strained voice. "Whit! Eugene! Come here! *Hurry!*"

Eugene and Dylan followed her voice. They ran up to her. Connie was still frozen in her tracks. The eyes had not drawn any closer to her, but she expected them to all pounce at once. Whit was the only one courageous enough to move forward. He borrowed Eugene's torch and extended it far out in front of him so he could see. With the walls illuminated, they realized what the "eyes" really were. The walls were covered with bright gold coins, coupled together so that they appeared to be eyes.

Dylan's jaw dropped. "LeRue's treasure!"

Whit studied the coins carefully and scratched his chin. There was something not right. "Maybe not," Whit said. "I don't think LeRue would be this obvious."

Eugene inched closer to the embedded coins, and his eyes lit up. "Mr. Whittaker, these coins appear to be Roman, twelfth century!"

This was enough for Dylan. He knew what treasure was, and twelfth-century coins were enough treasure for him. There had to be 200 coins in the room. Fifty of them would surely make him rich beyond his wildest dreams. He lunged for the wall. "Wow! These must be worth a fortune!" He grabbed a coin before Whit could protest.

Dylan pulled a coin away from the wall. Suddenly a loud creaking noise was heard behind the walls. It sounded as if the entire place was going to collapse. The floor became a trapdoor, sinking in the middle.

"Aaahh!" Connie screamed.

Eugene grabbed onto a rock jutting out from the wall.

"No, Dylan! Stop!" Whit shouted, grabbing Dylan's hand and holding it still. Dylan held the coin inches from the place where it had been embedded.

The creaking stopped, and the floor was still. Bits of dirt trickled into the hole that had once been solid ground. Eugene and Connie pressed up against the wall as close as they could manage. Dylan froze in fear.

Whit got up enough nerve to take a step, and he examined the coin in Dylan's hand. Attached to the back of the coin was a thin wire that led into the wall. Above the wire, Whit noticed that "Proverbs 26:27" was etched into the wall.

"Nobody move."

Nobody did.

"I think I know the proverb that's inscribed in this wall," said Whit. "'Whoever digs a pit will fall into it.'" Whit lifted his torch toward the ceiling and shed light on the inner workings of a booby trap. The wire from the wall led up to the ceiling, where it attached to a sophisticated system of gears, ropes, and pulleys. The gears rotated very slowly. Dirt trickled down and made some of the ropes move, causing the trapdoor to shake.

"Carefully replace the coin," Whit said to Dylan.

Dylan's hand slowly inched toward the wall. He pressed the coin back into its original spot. The creaking began again, startling all of them, but then they realized that the floor was closing up, returning to its original position.

Everyone breathed a sigh of relief. Eugene extracted his fingernails from the rock wall.

Whit stated the obvious. "These coins are rigged. Obviously LeRue is trying to weed out those who seek his treasure for selfish gain." Dylan felt ashamed. Mr. Whittaker was talking to him.

❋   ❋   ❋

Stanley stormed toward the cave entrance with a brand-new energy flowing through him. He gave his disobedient camel a dirty look and pushed it in the back. "Move aside, you sorry excuse for an animal."

His push barely moved the beast, but the camel did shift its weight. Without Stanley's knowledge, the camel stepped back onto the trigger pedestal as Stanley walked through the cave entrance.

"I've got you now, John Avery—"

The stone came to life, rolling slowly back over the hole. Stanley panicked, having instant visions of being stuck in this cave forever. He rushed back to the entrance but didn't make it. The stone rolled back just as his face extended past the doorway, and it squished his cheeks together.

"Whittaker," he said pitifully.

✳   ✳   ✳

It wasn't difficult for Whit to convince everyone to get out of the Hall of Coins and go back into the small chamber. No one wanted to tempt the floor to collapse again. "I don't think LeRue would have rigged anything harmful, but we still have to be careful. Remember, these caves are ancient and possibly unstable." He stood before the chamber wall and pointed at it. "Before we ran into that cavern, I noticed this message written on the wall." It was another French inscription.

Connie stepped forward quickly. "Here, let me try to translate. 'Many have sought . . .' something . . . 'but entrance will be . . .' something. That's all I got."

"Always helpful," Eugene said with a wry smile, stepping forward to take a real shot at a translation. "Actually, the message is another rhyme. It reads 'Many have sought the hidden keys, but entry is only to one of these.'"

The word *entry* led them all to look at a tiny hole in the wall. "That's the entrance?" Dylan said. "You're all too big. There's no way you could fit through that."

Whit scratched his chin. "'Entry to one of these' . . . I wonder . . . " His eyes lit up. "Of course! That's got to be it!"

"Did I miss something?" Connie asked.

"It's a reference to the book of Matthew! The part where Jesus teaches that only if you become like one of these little ones will you enter the kingdom of God. It illustrates how we must depend on God for everything—just like a baby depends on his parents. This has got to be the correct passageway!"

"But I'm the only one small enough to go in," Dylan said.

"Well, what are you waiting for?" Connie asked.

"Yessss!" Dylan declared, proud that he was able to contribute something to this quest. He dove for the hole.

"No, Dylan! Wait!" Mr. Whittaker shouted. He wanted to check first to make sure the structure was stable enough. But Dylan was in before Whit could even close his mouth.

"It's all right, Mr. Whittaker," Dylan said from inside the wall. "I'll be careful."

*　　*　　*

Stanley finally got a break when the camel stepped on the pedestal again. Otherwise, his face might have been stuck in the cave entrance for good. The camel's back foot triggered the pedestal, and the stone rolled back away from the entrance. Stanley felt his jaw to make sure it was still in one piece, then tested all the major elements of his mouth—lips, teeth, tongue—and all seemed to be working properly.

He pulled the camel's reins to move the animal away from the pedestal and scolded it again. "OK, now stay! Don't move from this spot. I don't want you anywhere near that peg over there! So stay, you ugly, smelly, dirty animal. Stay!" He slowly crept backward into the cave entrance, keeping a close eye on the camel.

Unfortunately, that meant he wasn't watching where he was going. When his foot met the trip wire, he was swept off his feet, and he flipped up to the ceiling. A rope was tied around his leg. He stayed there for a moment, suspended upside down, swinging slightly. The camel was still standing at the cave entrance. Stanley sighed. "Here, camel, camel. Here, nice camel."

the caves of qumran

The camel backed away and hit the pedestal. The cave entrance shut.

* * *

Dylan found himself enclosed in complete darkness until Eugene handed him the torch through the hole in the wall. He turned in a full circle with the torch to make sure there was nothing and no one in there with him. It was another passageway, and the only other living thing was a spider.

"Creepy," he said. He followed the spider with the light of his torch as it crawled along the side of the wall. It stopped near a lever, which disappeared into the rock.

Whit called in. "Dylan, are you OK in there?"

"Yeah, Mr. Whittaker. I found a lever." Dylan's voice sounded like it was inside a barrel. Dylan pushed the lever, and for a few seconds nothing happened.

Eugene, Connie, and Whit peered in through the hole, trying to see what was going on.

Suddenly they heard something outside the hole. They looked up as a deep, muted moan filled the passageway. The cave wall behind them creaked to life and then came open, releasing a flurry of bats. They darted out of the wall with a piercing sound, like car tires screeching to a stop. Thinking quickly, Connie reached into her backpack and pulled out a monstrous umbrella. It popped open, shielding all of them from the bats. The creatures skimmed the top of the umbrella like enormous raindrops, then headed back down the passageway and away from the gang. Everyone waited until the bats were all out of sight, and then Connie closed the umbrella. They all breathed a sigh of relief.

Eugene stared at Connie quizzically, then finally spoke. "You brought an umbrella to the desert?"

❋   ❋   ❋

The blood was beginning to rush to Stanley's head, and he started to panic. He had been hanging upside down for several minutes now, and the more he struggled, the tighter the rope around his ankle got.

Rope!

Stanley had an idea. He reached into his vest pocket and pulled out a multipurpose Swiss Army knife. He had never used any part of it except for the toothpick, which he packed in case he needed to pick food out of his teeth. He pulled out a nail file, a tiny scissors that wouldn't cut through a blade of grass, a spoon, a fork, a corkscrew . . . ah! The knife.

He bent upward with difficulty and began to cut through the rope. It was difficult going, but as he made some headway he suddenly realized that when he cut through the rope, he would fall. The drop wasn't that far, but the rocks were quite hard, as he had already learned by getting his face squished between two of them. Still, he continued to cut, thread by thread, until there were only a few threads of rope left. He closed his eyes and prepared for the impact.

Thud! He landed in a heap. He was stunned for a moment. Then, with all the determination he could muster, he bounded up and gazed down the passageway. He decided that now he was mad.

"All right, Whittaker, you're more clever than I thought. You may think your little traps can stop me, but you've got to get up pretty early in the morning to slow down 'Stan the Man' Martin."

He marched down the passageway. "There isn't a danger I haven't stared down. Nothing, but nothing, scares Stanley Martin!"

He stopped when he heard a strange noise. A black cloud was coming toward him, and as it got closer, he realized it was a torrent of screeching bats! He ducked his head as the bats tore around him, through his hair, under his legs, around his back. "Aaaaahhhhhhhh!" He flailed his arms and legs about, wildly throwing himself in every direction. The bats passed by without attacking, but even after they were gone, he continued to tear his hands through his hair. "Get out of my hair! Go away!"

The screeching faded into the distance, and he took one last swipe with his hands to make sure there were no stragglers. He was breathing hard. He lifted the tape recorder to his lips: "Note to self: Update rabies shot."

✳   ✳   ✳

The black vehicle pulled up to the closed entrance of the cave. Rudy and Boris were in the front and Mr. X was in the back.

They spotted the five camels standing in front of the stone wall.

"They went in right there," Rudy said without much confidence. He and Boris exchanged looks. They thought they'd seen the group come this way, but how had the stone been moved away from the wall? Rudy wondered what kind of man this Whittaker person was, that he could vanish inside solid rock.

"Hey, Mr. X, how do you know this Whittaker fella?" Rudy asked.

Rudy could hear the smile in Mr. X's voice. "Let's just say we're old friends."

Boris tried to get a closer look at the wall to see if there was an opening. The camels were in the way. "Look at those boneheaded camels," he said. "Watch this." Boris lay on the horn, sending the camels scattering in all directions. He snickered at his immature prank, smacking Rudy on the shoulder. But Rudy wasn't laughing. He was watching as the stone rolled away from the cave entrance. One of the camels had stepped on the pedestal in its frenzy.

The cave was wide open, ready to be explored.

Mr. X rubbed his hands together. "Gentlemen, I believe we have some business to attend to."

five

The Angel Chamber

DYLAN CRAWLED out of the small hole, and they all peered into the doorway that had been revealed when Dylan pushed the lever. It opened into a large chamber. The torches lit up the walls, which were covered with drawings of swords, lamps, fountains of water, and fire. Eugene and Connie admired the drawings for their beauty. Whit appreciated the drawings as well but also saw a pattern in them. The drawings continued without a break until they reached a smooth wall in the back of the chamber. On this wall there was a drawing of an open book. They all stepped toward it and read the inscription on the open page of the book: "119.105."

"Mr. Whittaker, another clue?" Eugene asked.

"Could be," Whit said. "LeRue has a theme in this

room. Do you see it?" No one did. "Look around. The lamps, the swords, the pictures. They're all images that the Bible uses to describe the Word of God."

They all nodded their heads in agreement.

"And look at the inscription. '119.105.' I'm thinking that's a reference to Psalm 119, verse 105, which says—"

" 'Your word is a lamp to my feet and a light to my path,' " Connie interrupted. "I memorized that verse years ago."

"Exactly," Whit said, smiling. "So let's see. What clue can we take from that? Word? Lamp? Lamp. That could be it. Everyone look for a lamp of some kind."

The group spread out, searching the floor for anything resembling a lamp. Eugene scanned the walls, and there, hanging from its handle, was a teapot-shaped lamp.

"Mr. Whittaker, it appears that you are indeed correct."

Eugene reached for the lamp, and it tilted. Another rumble. Eugene stepped back from the wall, hesitant to move the lamp any more after the experience in the hall of coins. Connie glanced down to see if the floor was going to collapse. It didn't budge, but she backed up against the wall just in case. A small hole in the ceiling opened, and a thin beam of light shot into the room. The beam moved slowly toward the large Bible portrait. They all ducked away from the beam as it traveled across the floor.

Stanley followed the same path that Whit and the others had taken, and he found himself at the fork in the passageway. He saw the hole that Dylan had passed through and the hallway to the left. He went left. He could sense that he was close. Very close.

"All right, Whittaker, you can try to stop me with rabid bats or whatever else your fiendish little mind can come up with. But I promise you that nothing will distract me from . . . oooh. Gold coins." His eyes got bigger as he saw the large number of them embedded in the walls. *This must be LeRue's treasure,* Stanley thought. Apparently he had found it first. But even if the others had somehow missed this room, he knew Whittaker couldn't be far behind. He checked his pants' pockets to determine if there was enough room for all these coins, then decided to snatch as many as possible. He pulled the first one forcefully from the wall.

Before he could put it in his pocket, the floor dropped open and flipped him headfirst into the water underneath it. At the same moment, a lasso appeared from above and wrapped around his ankles, lifting him up out of the pool.

Stanley could not even get his bearings before he found himself hanging upside down from the ceiling once again. But something told him this time it was not over.

Gears cranked into action above him. He glanced up and saw a sophisticated pulley system start. His eyes scanned it and stopped on a track in the ceiling, which started at the rope and disappeared into the next room. He could predict what was next.

"Mother," he said in a pitiful voice.

The rope shook him up and down for a few seconds, then dragged him out of the room at blazing speed. Still upside down, he just missed the rock doorway as he sped past it. As if on an amusement park ride out of control, he was flung back and forth as the track went around dangerous curves and through tiny tunnels.

Careening down a long passageway, he looked ahead of him and appeared to be running headlong into a dead-end wall!

"Aaahhhhhh!"

He closed his eyes and prepared to be flattened. But at the last possible moment the wall slid away, and he roared beyond it. He breathed a momentary sigh of re-lief, hoping this ride was over.

He was wrong. Another pool of water loomed ahead, and Stanley was sure he was going to be dropped into it. Instead, the rope pulled him through the water, his head and shoulders creating a wake in the water like a motorboat would make.

The track shifted upward, and he was lifted from the water. He barely had time to shake the water out of his eyes and nose before he beheld his next misfortune. He plummeted toward two wooden boards that stuck out of the wall. He shivered to think what purpose they would have. He stopped, his back just inches from the boards. A few moments passed for him to contemplate what was coming.

"No, please, no."

The boards reared back and, as if Stanley's backside were a snare drum, they paddled him.

"Ow, ow, ow, ow, ow, ow . . ."

The rope came loose from the ceiling and dunked him into a pit of gooey molasses below. A couple of dips, and Stanley was covered in the sticky goo. The rope rotated him toward the cave wall, and the cave opened up, blowing out a blast of air and a truckload of feathers. They stuck on the molasses, turning Stanley into a massive, upside-down chicken.

Stanley wiped his face and dropped the coin from his hand—and began to cry.

❊   ❊   ❊

Mr. X and his men were hot on the trail. They ignored the hall of coins passageway and went straight for the doorway that led into the lamp chamber.

"Quickly, through that door," said Mr. X.

Whit and the others watched as the beam of light continued its way along the floor and caught the reflection of a
mirror. The mirror bounced the light to another mirror,
which bounced it to yet another mirror. This continued
until the entire room was filled with brilliant light.

"Fantastic," said Eugene.

"Whoa," said Dylan.

Connie snapped a photo.

The last beam landed on a magnifying glass and
shone onto a taut rope, which caused the rope to start
burning.

"That doesn't look good," said Connie. She snapped
another picture.

The rope frayed to only a few strands, and the four
braced themselves for whatever was coming. The rope
snapped, and a door at the far end of the room slowly
opened. The light from the mirrors lit the way into the
new room.

"Awesome!" Dylan said.

"Indeed," agreed Eugene.

They moved from the lamp chamber—just as the
beams from Rudy's flashlight shone in unnoticed.

The next chamber was covered with cobwebs. Whit
peeled back a veil from the doorway and everyone
stepped inside. They all stopped breathing momen-

tarily as they looked around at the grandeur. It was like a huge cathedral, with a towering ceiling and ornate architecture. Enormous tapestries with pictures of Christ hung from the walls, each of them depicting a different moment in Jesus' life. Relics from ancient times lay everywhere—statues, candelabras, and wooden crates with IXOYE carved into them.

But by far the most impressive object in this room was the 50-foot stone angel standing majestically over everything else in the room. Long velvet drapes hung behind the angel from ceiling to floor. The angel's arms were outstretched, and hanging from each arm, on suspended ropes like an ancient scale, were wooden platforms. On the platform hanging from the angel's right arm was a dusty old trunk. On the platform hanging from the angel's left arm was a treasure chest overflowing with gold medallions.

All eyes were on this wondrous sight.

Whit nodded. "The Angel Chamber. The legends are true."

Connie snapped a picture.

Dylan focused on the treasure chest. If gold medallions filled up the entire volume of that trunk, there had to be thousands of coins in it. The hall of coins could have made him rich. But the stuff in this place would make him a millionaire.

"Mr. Whittaker," Dylan exclaimed, "this is . . ."

"Excellent." A voice from behind finished his sentence. Everyone whirled around to see who had spoken, but the face was still hidden by darkness just outside the doorway.

"Excellent work, Whittaker," the voice continued.

Whit tried to place the voice. It finally came to him. "Faustus?"

Fred J. Faustus emerged from the shadows and stood before Whit. "Well, I see your memory hasn't gone."

Whit and Faustus had a history. Several years before, Faustus had stolen Mr. Whittaker's greatest invention, the Imagination Station. Whit designed it to allow children to relive history in their imaginations. But Faustus had taken it and tried to use it to manipulate the minds of children into believing evil lies. Mr. Whittaker had won that battle, but the war was obviously not over. Faustus was back, poised to thwart another of Mr. Whittaker's achievements.

Yet Whit still wasn't certain what was going on. "But . . . what are you doing here?"

"Isn't it obvious?" Faustus said, chuckling. "I'm here to claim my treasure."

Dylan stepped forward toward Faustus. He had been in the middle of the last battle with Faustus and knew of his treachery. "But the treasure is ours. I found the map!"

"Come now, boy. You actually think that the ancient

treasure map of Pierre LeRue just *appeared?* In Odyssey, of all places?"

A lightbulb went off in Whit's head. "You mean . . . you planted the map?"

"Well, actually, it was my men here who made the donation." Rudy and Boris stepped into the room and smiled.

"The donations to Whit's End!" Connie said.

"The movers!" Dylan said, pointing to Rudy and Boris.

Faustus let out a laugh, and Rudy and Boris joined in.

Whit asked, "And how, may I ask, did you get the map?"

"The easy way. I stole it! And who better to give it to than John Avery Whittaker. You see, I needed someone who possessed the biblical knowledge required to translate the clues. And now, thanks to you—"

"Everyone, hold it right there," came a voice from behind. It was Stanley Martin, covered in molasses and feathers from head to toe. Faustus smiled, amused that he was being threatened by a large chicken. Whit and the gang were confused by the presence of poultry in the chamber.

Faustus didn't appear the least bit threatened by Stanley's threat. "Oh no," he said, rolling his eyes, "you can't be serious."

Stanley blew off a tuft of feathers that had been hanging from his lip. "Don't I look serious?"

Connie snapped a photo.

Faustus turned his attention back to Whit. "Allow me to introduce Stanley D. Martin."

Stanley whipped out a silver badge. "Chief investigator of the International Association of Artifact Recovery. A powerful Washington-based agency."

"He's the only member," said Faustus.

"That may be so. But I was able to uncover Whittaker's diabolical plot, wasn't I?"

"Make no mistake, Mr. Martin. You are here only because I tipped you onto Whittaker's trail."

"But why?" Whit asked.

"I didn't just need your knowledge, Whittaker. I also needed someone to take the fall for this crime, and Martin swallowed the bait perfectly. When the authorities finally discover what's left of this little expedition, they'll think that Martin successfully caught you red-handed."

"And that's exactly what happened!" Stanley said proudly.

"But unfortunately," Faustus continued, "there will have been a small cave-in that trapped you all inside. The authorities will sadly presume the treasure to be lost once and for all. Meanwhile, I will have gotten away scot-free!"

Stanley's feathered brow rumpled. He was confused. The bad guy had suddenly changed. Faustus was about to trap them all inside a cave. Whittaker was only trying to find the same treasure Stanley was looking for. Was it true that Faustus had stolen the map, not Whittaker? It was too much for Stanley to grasp at this moment, so he chose desperation. "What are you talking about? Now would everyone please step away from the treasure?"

Faustus had an impatient look on his face. "Gentlemen, Mr. Martin has served his purpose. Would you please dispose of him before he molts?"

Rudy and Boris moved toward Stanley. He protested. "Not until I get to the bottom of—oof!" Rudy and Boris picked him up by the armpits and pinned him against the wall.

"Thank you, gentlemen. Now please, someone translate the final clue, or my friends will make things most uncomfortable for Mr. Martin."

Whit nodded at Eugene, and he approached the huge French inscription on the wall. He cleared his throat and began. "Two treasures hang before your eyes. The proper choice strengthens the wise. One gives you more from day to day. The other consumes and fades away."

"What is that supposed to mean?" Faustus asked. "Whittaker, solve the riddle."

"So far, the clues have been based on Scripture. Jesus

taught that the things of this world, such as the gold coins in that chest there, will fade away. The coins, then, would be the foolish choice." He turned toward the dusty trunk at the angel's right. "So that trunk must contain the treasure."

Faustus grunted. "It's always a moral issue with you, isn't it, Whittaker? Regardless, it is a clever idea to hide the greatest riches in an old, dusty trunk. Now be a gent and retrieve the trunk for your old friend."

Whit stepped forward to obey. Connie reached out and grabbed Whit's arm. She whispered, "You're not actually going along with him, are you, Whit?"

Whit whispered back, "Connie, it's not worth risking the safety of the three of you."

Stanley was still pinned to the wall. "Don't cave in to him, Whittaker," he managed to say.

Whit walked up to lower the ropes. He untied the rope from the wall and let the rope slip through his hands. The angel's right arm and the pallet slowly inched toward the ground. It was only seconds until they would behold the great treasure of Pierre LeRue.

six

The Greatest Treasure

STANLEY STRUGGLED and whined. Rudy and Boris barely moved as he thrashed around in their grasp.

As the angel's arm lowered, the walls creaked. Dust fell from the ceiling. Whit looked up, concerned.

Faustus was tired of the blubbering. "Take him away," he said, pointing to Stanley. "Then come back and help me with this treasure!"

Rudy and Boris quickly escorted Stanley out, even though they really wanted to stay and see the treasure.

Dylan didn't know how to feel about the treasure. He was confused by everything that had happened so far. All the clues seemed to be teaching a lesson about not being greedy for money, but then, what could possibly be more valuable than all those gold medallions? *Perhaps this was a test to prove that since we made it this far we're really not greedy,* he thought, *and there's a gigantic diamond in this trunk as our prize.* But now, with Faustus there, he didn't believe he would ever see the diamond anyway. Perhaps he would never even see the light of day. Somehow, with his life on the line, the riches didn't seem all that important anymore. Dylan was still curious to know what was in the trunk, but frankly, he would now be disappointed if it did contain a gigantic diamond. There were other things more important.

The pallet reached the ground. Before Mr. Whittaker could move to open the trunk, Faustus brushed past him and slid on his knees in front of it, as if he were worshiping it. "Finally, it's mine! Fame! Riches! Fortune!" He hastily opened the trunk and discovered—

A book. Faustus fished around in the bottom of the trunk some more, frantically searching for anything else, but it was empty. The book was all there was.

"A book? What is this nonsense, Whittaker?" He spun around on his heels and shoved the book into Mr. Whittaker's stomach, immediately turning to the platform still hanging from the angel's left arm. "I should've known you'd foul this up."

Whit looked down at the book in his hands as Connie, Eugene, and Dylan approached. The cover read *La Bible.*

"La Bible," Whit said.

Whit smiled. "Of course! Our greatest treasure is the Bible! Pierre knew that gold and riches lead to destruction. The key to the kingdom of God is found only in the riches of his Word. The Word of God!"

Dylan wasn't disappointed.

Faustus, however, was. "You can keep your antiquated book, Whittaker. I won't be so foolish!" He strode off for the other chest.

"Faustus, no! You might bring this whole place down on us!"

Faustus yanked the rope from the wall and let it slide through his fingers. The platform fell to the ground quickly. The gold glinted majestically in the light. Faustus sifted through the precious gold with his fingers, laughing in delight. But filling a few bags with gold would not be enough for him. He had to take the whole chest.

"Mr. Faustus, no!" Eugene shouted. "The cave's not stable!"

"And neither are you if you think I'm just going to leave all this here."

Not waiting for Rudy and Boris to come back, he lifted the chest off the platform. The platform began to rise back up to its former position. The arms of the angel tilted like an unbalanced scale. A low rumbling came from behind the walls.

"Faustus, stop! This is insane! You're putting all of us in danger! You're being controlled by your greed."

"Call it what you will, Whittaker. But it will get me a lot farther than your silly ideals ever will."

Suddenly, the only door leading out of the chamber shut tight. Faustus stopped in his tracks. The rumbling continued, only louder. It grew more and more thunderous until the walls began to crumble.

But they had a bigger problem. Whit looked up at the crumbling walls. "Connie, Dylan, Eugene—look out!"

Out of the wall burst hundreds of gallons of water. It came at them as if it were pouring out a dam that had been poked through. Connie and Dylan ran, but Eugene had a better idea.

"Follow me!" he said, looking up at the empty platform.

❊   ❊   ❊

Rudy and Boris dragged Stanley quickly down the passageway toward the cave entrance. Unaware of the latest crisis, they figured they were missing all the fun of seeing and touching the treasure. They would take Stanley to another part of the cave and tie him up until they decided what to do.

Stanley pleaded with them. "Please don't hurt me. I have a small hamster at home. His name is Elvis. He needs me. I only put a week's worth of food in his cage; he'll just waste away to nothing if I don't get back." He was so busy blubbering that he didn't notice that they'd stopped. Boris looked up. The entire cave shook and gravel fell from the ceiling.

"Did you hear that?" said Boris. Rudy nodded. They listened intently. It sounded as if the entire cave was going to collapse around them.

"Yeah, let's get outta here. Looks like this is your lucky day, Martin." They dropped him on the ground and ran for the exit.

Stanley was momentarily stunned, but he quickly regained his composure. *Of course,* he thought. *They probably realized they were no match for me.* He called after them. "Yeah, you run away! Next time maybe you'll think twice before messing with Stan Martin!"

He spun around and looked back down the hall toward the Angel Chamber.

※　　※　　※

Whit grabbed the Bible and placed it in his waterproof knapsack. The gushing water was covering the floor and getting deeper by the second. A fierce wave of water dislodged two large rocks right at Connie's feet. The room sprung leaks all over.

Faustus knew he would have no chance if he tried to lug the entire treasure chest out of the cave. He dropped to his knees and used his hands to scoop as many gold coins as he could into a canvas bag. As the canvas bag grew very heavy with each handful of coins, it became obvious that his greed was still too impractical.

Eugene climbed onto the platform, causing the angel's arm to creak downward slightly. He wasn't heavy enough to stop the water. "I need more weight!" he yelled. He reached down and grabbed for Connie, who was swimming just below him. With a full-out stretch from Eugene and a desperate lunge from Connie, he managed to grasp her wrist and pull her onto the platform with him. The angel's arm creaked down a little farther and locked into place. The water stopped pouring in.

Connie screamed with delight. "You're all witnesses! Never let it be said that I am not the perfect weight!"

Snap!

The rope holding the platform broke, plunging Eugene and Connie into the pool. The water resumed pouring into the room.

The water level reached the height of the exit door, which was still closed, but Faustus desperately swam for it anyway. His bag of coins made it very difficult, because the weight kept pulling him underwater. He flailed around, using all the strength he had to stay afloat.

✳   ✳   ✳

Dylan, Eugene, Connie, and Whit were flopping around in six feet of treacherous water. Dylan shouted, banging on the door. "Help! Somebody, help!"

"Is somebody out there?" Whit asked.

Connie put her ear to the door, hoping to hear some-one on the other side.

Everyone screamed. "Let us out! Get us out of here! Help!"

The rushing water was deafening. Dylan and Whit swam over to a wall and climbed onto it, their hands grasping at ridges in the cave wall. Dylan climbed up on Whit's shoulders.

Below them, Faustus clung to a floating wooden crate that was slowly coming apart. The weight of the gold coins was too much for the small crate to handle. It pulled him under. "Nooooooo!"

The bag submerged him and the water muffled his desperate cry. But still he refused to let go of his new fortune. Bubbles floated upward from his mouth.

Connie and Eugene floated on a wooden pallet. They could barely see anything anymore because the water from the ceiling had extinguished all but one torch flame, the one held by Eugene. Connie pulled out her flashlight just as a torrent of water smashed into their makeshift raft, causing her to drop her backpack.

"Oh no! My backpack!" It sank beneath the water.

"Miss Kendall, this is hardly the time to be thinking of such meaningless things," Eugene said.

Connie nodded. "You're right. That's totally unimportant right now."

A chunk of rock from the ceiling fell into the water with a splash that completely soaked them.

"Oh no! My hair!" Connie said with a sigh.

Her backpack had settled on the chamber floor. Also on the chamber floor and quickly running out of breath was Faustus, still struggling with his weighty treasure. It stood firm, as if it were a tree he was trying to pull out of the ground.

✱   ✱   ✱

Stanley stood 15 feet from the stone door, rearing back and ready to break through the solid rock. He lowered his shoulder and ran full force toward the door, screaming. *Smack!* He was on his back in milliseconds, as stiff as a board.

✱   ✱   ✱

The water flowed in faster than ever. The depth had everyone floating two feet away from the ceiling. Whit and Dylan still clung to the rock wall. Dylan had to bend his head over to duck under the ceiling.

Whit saw all the horror around him and took a moment to pray. "Please, dear Lord, save us."

Eugene held the last torch as a trickle of water

dripped from the ceiling and extinguished the flame. "Oh, my," he said in the dark.

Suddenly his face was flooded with light as Connie aimed her flashlight at him. "I told you this would come in handy. See? Waterproof."

✳   ✳   ✳

Stanley stood up awkwardly, swaying back and forth. He saw all kinds of stars—entire constellations—after hitting the stone door. But his determination didn't wane. He lifted a wobbly finger. "All right," he said with difficulty, "I'll give you to the count of three. One . . ." He failed to notice a small crack in the stone doorway. He lifted another finger. "Two . . ." Still dazed from smacking into the door, he stared at his fingers, going blank as to what came next. Water trickled in through the cracks in the door. "Oh. Three!"

Suddenly the door disintegrated, and a torrent of water burst through and swept him off his feet.

From inside the Angel Chamber, the water rushed out the open door and, like a big whirlpool, spun everyone inside the room toward the exit. Before any of them knew what was happening, they were all sucked out the door and into the tunnel at horrific speeds.

Stanley had no idea what had just happened, but he found himself careening down a narrow passageway.

He spotted a slab of wood floating near him, lunged for it, and pulled himself on top of it, struggling to keep his balance.

Flying down the hallway like an out-of-control indoor roller coaster, Eugene and Connie managed to climb back onto the floating platform. Whit was driven into a cave wall but got his bearings and spotted them. He scrambled onto the platform with their help. Using Connie's flashlight as a headlight, they kept an eye on the stone walls that rushed toward them at every turn. Whit also kept an eye out for Dylan. He thought he saw him just up ahead.

Dylan was probably the least fazed of anyone by all of this. He surfed on a piece of wood, riding up the high waves, ducking his head under the narrow passageways. He made a radical cut straight up the side of the cave and down again.

"Yes!" he shouted, pumping his fist.

The tunnel got wider, and the river Dylan was on joined another. From the other river, Stanley rode up to meet him. He was surfing, wobbly-kneed, on the piece of wood, still struggling to keep his balance but gaining in confidence. Dylan was surprised to see him. "Mr. Martin?"

"Hey, kid," said Stanley, still sparsely covered in feathers. Some of them had blown or washed off. He smiled at Dylan. "I think I'm getting the hang of this." He gave him the "hang loose" sign and wondered if he should try to show off and raise one foot off the substitute surfboard.

He didn't have time to add to his performance because Eugene yelled at him from behind, "Mr. Martin, watch out!"

Stanley's eyes widened. Sticking up through the water was a stalagmite, like an upside-down icicle, dead ahead. He had learned how to turn, but it was too late. The pointed rock split his wooden surfboard in half. Stanley continued on two water skis. He panicked and started to fall, but Dylan cut in behind and caught him, lifting him back upright.

Eugene heard a rumble and turned around. A furious tidal wave pounded the walls behind him. It was gaining on them. Eugene lay prostrate on the raft, paddling frantically with his arms to propel them forward. The tidal wave still gained ground.

"Don't look now, but we're in for a little bump," said Connie, watching nervously ahead of her.

The river dropped into a deep hole, and there straight before them was an enormous waterfall. Eugene paddled the other direction, but it was too little, too late.

"Aaaaahhhhhh!" they all screamed as they plummeted down the steep waterfall. The tidal wave plunged after them. The wood slipped out from underneath them, and they were thrown into the water.

Thrashed about by rushing water, Dylan couldn't find the surface. He panicked and looked around for something to grab. There was nothing. He kicked and floated upward. Suddenly he saw a bright light over him. He frantically swam toward it, feeling like his lungs would burst any minute. The light got brighter and brighter as he continued to pump his arms and legs forcefully. He could make out a blue sky, trees, and finally camels. The surface came to meet him.

Sploosh! He broke the surface and gasped for breath. He was in an oasis. He scrambled for the shore of the small body of water. He lunged for the side and pulled himself up onto the sand. The five camels were gathered around, drinking. No one else was there. *What happened to everyone else?* Dylan wondered.

In seconds, he got his answer. One by one, like gophers, the heads of his friends popped out of the water. Stanley popped out too. They all gasped for breath and swam to the shore. For a few moments they all clung to the sand and coughed up water. The whole crew was safe.

Dylan glanced around. "We made it!" he shouted, pumping his fist again in the air. "Yeah!"

"Is everybody OK?" Whit asked.

Still not quite recovered, everyone nodded. Stanley laughed, and everyone else joined in. They had made it.